T0132250

Flash's Life

Charlie Alexander

Flash's Life

Written by Charlie Alexander
Artwork by Charlie Alexander

Flash added Charlie's books to the library.

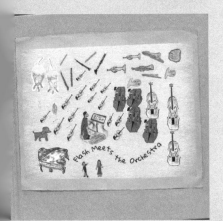

There were lots of them!

New books arriving today.

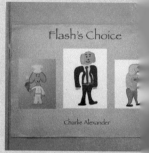

Flash has a library card.

Putting all these books away was a big job.

But Flash loved putting all the stories of himself on the shelf.

Flash was involved with many sports.

He was good at most of them!

Flash participates in any sport.

He always makes his life full of fun!

These are more sports that Flash liked.

Flash loved his life!

Flash's life is vey active.

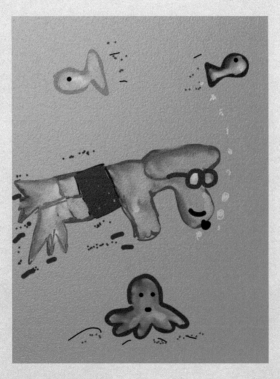

He learned how to play so many games.

Flash loves to play golf.

Even if it rains!

Swimming with the fish was so cool!

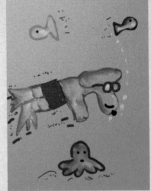

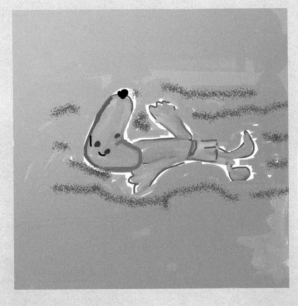

Flash had more than a few bathing suits.

Flash likes lots of boats too!

Rowing and splashing and seeing a whale make boating an exciting pleasure for Flash.

Flash graduated from high school.

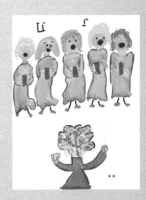

He also earned a college degree. Education was so important in his life.

It was up to Flash to choose what he liked.

There were lots of careers he liked.

Flash kept finding new jobs to do.

He always stays busy and happy.

There were so many choices.

Flash enjoyed trying all of them!

Flash sure knew how to work!

He does so many different things.

Fancy is so important to Flash.

He loves her with all his heart!

A big part of Flash's life is music.

And Piano is his most favorite instrument!

Playing the piano is the best!

Flash was in a world of his own!

All instruments meant a lot to Flash.

He liked trying each one!

Flash enjoyed his days at the park.

He really flipped over all the rides!

Flash liked all the birds, fish and alligators.

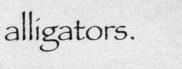

In fact, Flash loved all the animals.

Flash knows staying busy is a good thing.

Some days just flew by.

Trick or treat!

Great costumes and candy

waiting.

He also piloted planes and helicopters
and even the space shuttle.

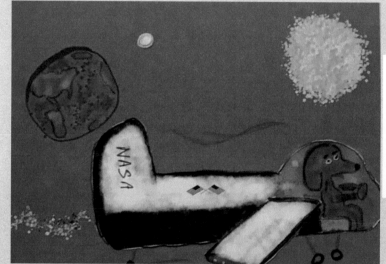
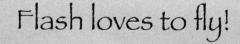

Flash loves to fly!

Flash lifted off!

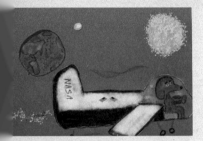

He was soon in orbit and weightless.

Flash landed back on earth.

Working on the farm was something Flash enjoyed

Flash drove many times in his life.

There were cars, trucks and buses!

Lunch was always Flash's favorite part of the day.

There were so many treats to enjoy!

Flash couldn't wait for lunch on most days!

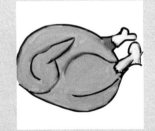

It was fun to take a lunch break anytime.

There were always fun things to do.

Every day presented lots of fun activities!

Traveling all over the world was so wonderful.

Flash's life took him to so many places!

Flash even had a chance to be a cowboy.

Flash loved riding and roping!.

All the animals were friends too.

Flash loved them all!

All of these animals thought Flash was very caring.

Flash loved each of his friends!

Church was very important to Flash.

His life was filled with family and prayers.

Sleeping late was a pleasure for Flash.

It didn't happen very often!

Flash's Life is exciting!! Especially with family!

Flash enjoys every second!
The End

To order additional copies of this book, contact:
Xlibris
844-714-8691
www.Xlibris.com
Orders@Xlibris.com

ISBN: Softcover   978-1-6698-7717-2
           Hardcover   978-1-6698-7718-9
           EBook   978-1-6698-7716-5

Library of Congress Control Number: 2023908763

Print information available on the last page

Rev. date: 05/10/2023

Printed in the United States
by Baker & Taylor Publisher Services